Augustavus Nicholas Nichols

Mildred Eagleton and Other Good and Bad Ballads

Augustavus Nicholas Nichols

Mildred Eagleton and Other Good and Bad Ballads

ISBN/EAN: 9783744787758

Printed in Europe, USA, Canada, Australia, Japan

Cover: Foto ©Andreas Hilbeck / pixelio.de

More available books at **www.hansebooks.com**

MILDRED EAGLETON,

AND OTHER GOOD AND

BAD BALLADS;

BY

AUGUSTAVUS NICHOLAS NICHOLS,

AUTHOR OF

"ˍINKY BELL," "ALPHONSE AND ETHELBERTA,"
"THE APOSTLES' SCREED," "AN EMBAR-
RASSING SITUATION," "BIBLE BABBLE,"
ETC., ETC., ETC.

From grave to gay, from lively to SEVERE.—*Very old English.*

REPRINTED FROM THE LATEST LONDON EDITION, WITH ALTERATIONS AND ADDITIONS.

CHICAGO:
PUBLISHED BY
DODDER, NICHOLS AND FAGG,
MDCCCLXXXVIII.

CONTENTS.

THE AUTHOR TO HIS BOOK.

Go, little book that I have penned,
If here and there some fearless friend
Of honest thoughts shall turn to thee
And smile, it is enough for me.
Or, if he sigh, and kindly blame,
I prize his greeting quite the same ;
I only ask that he shall be
True to a large humanity.

True to that generous love which holds
All creatures in its ample folds,
That love which made man less forlorn
Long ages ere a creed was born ;
That love whose radiance, pure and warm,
Has lived through centuries of storm,
And shall attain a wider sway
When sects and creeds have passed away.

Go, little book, and do not shrink
From what men think, or say they think,—
For what men think and what they say
Are different oft, as night and day.
Alas ! for those with wills so weak
They bravely feel but feebly speak,—
Who know the truth, yet live and die
All tattooed over with a lie.

If none shall love thee, little book,
If none bestow a gentle look,—
If, like some tramp, thou findst each door
Is shut,—but no, thy varied store
Will not suggest the vagrant thief ;
To some thy visit will be brief,
But thou shalt be content to wait,
A smiling peddler at the gate.

Go, ring the bell, unpack thy rhymes,
A mirror of the moods and times
In which my fancies sang to me,—
Go say what I have said to thee.
Fear not,—what thy small bulk contains,
A motley lot of tangled skeins,
But symbolize, in lack of plan,
The twisting, tortuous mind of man.

The world is changing in its thought,—
Old creeds are dying with dry-rot;
Blind faith gives place to wholesome doubt,
And bigot fires are fizzling out.
With looser reins from their high perch
Its drivers urge the lumbering church,—
Who has not seen a parson choke
Over some good blasphemous joke?

A father's blessing now I give,—
I somehow feel that thou shalt live;
For thou art not too saintly mild,—
The imp survives the angelic child.
Go, join the circus, seek the strife,
An emblem thou of human life,—
Some pages merry and some sad,
A mixture strange of good and bad.

Haste, little traveler, on thy way,
Acquaintance make without delay,
For, let thy pace be slow or fast,
Oblivion yawns for thee at last.
And ere thy pilgrimage shall end
If here and there thou hast a friend,
'Tis well; as toward our graves we crawl,
But few do better, after all.

MILDRED EAGLETON.

Oh, dainty Mildred Eagleton,
  I know not where you be,
Among the hills of Switzerland,
  Or on the Indian sea,
But my love, my prayers do follow,
  Though you may not care for me.

And when your noble cavalier,
  Across the restless main,
Shall bring you to these pleasant skies
  And this bright land again,
I would have you read my story
  With pity, not with pain.

Oh, dainty Mildred Eagleton,
  I know when you were born ;
The rain beat down the lilacs,
  And bent the bladed corn
That stormy night, but Heaven did break
  Upon the world that morn.

For in the wind and in the rain
  A little bird did sing,
A little bird from Paradise,
  With love beneath its wing,
To build a nest within our hearts
  And make them breathe of Spring.

A little blossom of delight,
  Which some angelic hand
Let fall upon this barren earth,
  At God's benign command,
An emblem of the flowers that grew
  In that immortal land.

At first, those tiny baby hands,
  Rose-colored, like sea shells,
Could scarcely crush the violets
  To rob them of their smells,
Or shake the trembling drops from out
  The lilies' spangled bells.

But by-and-by you were so tall,
  Your eyes of sunny blue
Just peeped above the rose-bush
  That in the garden grew,
And then the early holly-hocks
  Were not so tall as you.

All hearts turned toward you, for it was
  A joyous thing to see
Such goodness growing on the earth,
  Where sin and sorrow be,
And every day your beauteous face
  Was more and more to me.

I was your gallant lover then,
  My heart beat proud and high
When you were kind, at your command
  No slave more meek than I ;
But the gossips looked askance and shook
  Their heads. I knew not why.

At last I left my home and you,
  By cruel duty sent
To lands of Saracen and Turk,
  To Arab mosque and tent,
But the thought of Millie Eagleton
  Dwelt with me where I went.

Across wild seas of sand I rode
  With dusty caravans,
And when in some infrequent pool
  I cast a curious glance,
I saw no youth's romantic face,
  But a bronzed and bearded man's.

Then I would pluck, with furtive hand,
  A picture from my breast,
And kiss the image of those lips
  I had so often pressed,—
It was the crucifix to which
  I all my love confessed.

Oh, often in the breathless night,
  Beneath those Orient skies,
I though of you, I dreamed of you,
  And with a thousand sighs
I blessed you for your bonny mouth,
  And for your gentle eyes.

Time fled, and I had gold enough
  To last for many a year ,
I yearned to see my native land,
  Its Sabbath bells to hear,
And to live the dream that I had dreamed,
  With one to me so dear.

Again I saw the chalky cliffs
  Rise from the purple sea,
We swept across the harbor bar
  With the south wind blowing free ;
We passed the lighthouse and the fort,
  And the sailors sang with glee.

Oh, how the blood leaped in my veins,
  And how my fond heart beat,
As I sped across the old stone bridge
  To your garden gate, my sweet,—
The gossips stared, as the sunburnt man
  Strode through the narrow street.

Ah, dainty Mildred Eagleton,
  I found you grown more fair ;
A deeper crimson touched your lips,
  And a darker gold your hair;
But over all, like an unseen veil,
  Was drawn such a queenly air.

When I left you for those foreign climes,
　　You were but a child, I know ;
A woman now, more lovely far,
　　But I scarce would have it so,
For I dared not hold you on my knee,
　　As I used to, long ago.

Oh, tell me, Mildred Eagleton,
　　If you remember still
The woodlands that we rambled through,
　　And the broken down old mill,
And the pebbly brook you waded in
　　At the foot of Stratham Hill ?

I've seen the ancient cities
　　That lie across the sea,
And crumbling column and broken arch
　　Told tales in a minor key.
But the ruined mill near Stratham Hill
　　Is a sweeter thought to me.

But let that pass.　I sat and talked
　　Of sights that I had seen,
To please your father, good old man,
　　With his locks of silvery sheen,—
Of dim seraglios of the East,
　　And the tomb of Egypt's queen.

And then I showed the trinkets
　　That I had brought for you,
The lucent garnets, hearts of fire,
　　And the opal's frozen dew,
And a necklace, that would match so well
　　With a pair of eyes I knew.

Then said your father, holding them
　　Above your blessed head,
"You shall not wear them, Millie dear,
　　Until the day you wed.
The Earl will thank you, Ralph, for these."
　　" The Earl ! the Earl !"　I said.

Oh, God ! that broke the dream I dreamt
  For many a tiresome year ;
I loved you, Mildred Eagleton,
  My soul was not so dear
As the little agate ear-ring
  That glimmered at your ear.

I loved you, Mildred Eagleton,
  God pardon me, that I
Had let that earthly love come in
  Between me and the sky,
But I loved you, Mildred Eagleton,
  With a love that could not die.

And when, upon that morn in May,
  I heard your marriage bell,
Methought an angel up in Heaven
  Was singing to me, in hell.
'Twas a chime for the Earl and a dirge for me,
  That the sexton rang so well.

I saw you, in your bridal robe,
  Come down the village street,
And laughing children strewed the way
  With pinks and roses sweet ;—
I would that I had been a flower,
  To perish at your feet.

Then, all the world grew strangely dark,
  I prayed that I might die ;
No wretch condemned to cruel death
  Ere begged for life as I
That God would give me rest with those
  Who in the churchyard lie.

When you were gone, and salt waves rolled
  Between your home and you,
I lingered near the dear old place
  That we in childhood knew ;
Some memory of my boyish love
  Each object brought to view.

At night, when other lids succumbed
   To slumber's gentle weight,
I paced, a silent sentinel,
   Outside your garden gate,
And lived again that happy dream
   From which I woke so late.

Let others tell how one wild night,
   Just as I turned away,
I saw a ruddy flame shoot out
   And on the darkness play,
Great God! it was the room in which
   Your helpless father lay.

I know not how I scaled the wall
   And through the casement broke,
No barrier, for a moment, stood
   Against my frenzied stroke ;
Like some fierce fiend I rushed into
   The blinding flame and smoke.

The household woke and fought the fire,
   Stirred by my loud alarm,
But I had saved your father's life,—
   I bore him on my arm
As he had been a sleeping babe,
   Beyond the reach of harm.

What matter that the angry flame
   Had stung me with its breath ?
God has been good, I did not dream
   To die so brave a death ;
With blessings all unsought, our prayers
   He sometimes answereth.

Upon my dying bed, my love
   Grows stronger day by day ;
Your father comes and blesses me,
   And trains my lips to pray ;
But sweeter still, I feel that you
   Will bless me, far away.

Oh, darling Millie Eagleton,
  I know not where you be,
Among the groves of Italy,
  Or on the southern sea,
But I bless you with my dying thoughts
  For what you've been to me.

When in the quiet grave I lie,
  With your picture on my breast,
Perhaps my soul may find repose
  In the mansions of the blest,
Where sorrow cannot enter,
  And the weary are at rest.

But when the vines of summer
  Above my grave shall curl,
Will you sometime stand beside me there,
  And say to your noble earl,
Here lies a hapless man who knew
  And loved me when a girl?

God bless you, Millie Eagleton,
  God bless the man who won
The fairest hand, the purest heart,
  There are beneath the sun
And let the bliss that I have missed
  Be his till life is done.—
God save us, every one!

THE WASH-WOMAN OVER THE WAY.

A SKETCH OF AN ECCENTRIC FAMILY.

There's a famous old wash-woman over the way,
  Her age I can hardly declare ;
She was not at all young in my grandfather's day,
She is toothless and deaf, her thin hair has turned gray,
Her once strapping figure is bent with decay,
  And her visage quite furrowed with care.

Yet still she keeps washing with might and with main,
  As if with some rival to cope ;
In a fluid whose nature I cannot explain
She plungeth her duds, flecked with many a stain,
And she rubbeth, and groaneth, and seemeth in pain,
  And is constantly calling for "soap!"

Her customers rally from far and from near,
  And appear to have faith in her skill ;
Though they notice, of course, the old woman is queer,
And consider her charges remarkably dear,
She has washed for their families year after year,
And partly from habit, and partly from fear,
  They depend on her services still.

Ay, the old dame can threaten, and sometimes she swears
  With an unction which few can withstand.
If one of her patrons imprudently dares
To transfer his custom, she fiercely declares
He is destined to roast when his earthly affairs
  Have slipped like an hour-glass of sand.

While others, who pay her exorbitant fees,
  In Heaven are quite certain to dwell ;
She thinks of both places she carries the keys,
That Jehovah must ratify all her decrees,
That her friends are to bask in perpetual ease,
  And her foes to be tortured in hell.

The artful old creature assumes to be meek,
   But her orders are selfish and mean ;
Her regular wash-day occurs once a week,
And then though amusement or rest you might seek,
You must march to her wash-house and list to the creak
   Of her rusty, old-fashioned machine.

She's so cross, if an urchin in passing should grin,
   She gives him a taste of her jaw ;
She gnasheth her gums and she waggeth her chin,
And she vows she will catch him and take off his skin,
A punishment fixed for his horrible sin
   By the ancient Levitical law.

This hag in her youth had a powerful voice,
   But now it is hopelessly cracked ;
She hums many tunes, yet she only employs
The doggrel of some of her worshipful boys,
Describing her beauty, her virtues and joys,
   More based upon fancy than fact.

All the while she keeps washing with might and with main,
   As if with some rival to cope ;
In a fluid whose nature I cannot explain
She plungeth her duds, flecked with many a stain,
And she rubbeth, and groaneth, and seemeth in pain,
   And is constantly calling for " soap ! "

She has numerous sons, and, regardful of looks,
   They humor their mother's wild whims ;
Her family pictures they cram in all nooks,
Old worm-eaten relics adorn shelves and hooks,
With skull-bones and crosses to scare off the spooks ;
They profess to believe her old sorcery books,
To relish the nauseous messes she cooks,
   And delight in her favorite hymns.

But while in attentions quite filial they seem
   And alert to her slightest behests,
They privately go to the other extreme ;

They sneak in the pantry and drink all the cream,
Go to ride in the park with the old woman's team,
And are always contriving, by some sort of scheme,
    To feather their personal nests.

Though each is supposed in the labor to share,
    They are sadly accustomed to shirk ;
They try to assume a superior air,
They are wasteful of '' soap,'' at the ladies they stare,
And are often conducting some raffle or fair,
    And thereby neglecting their work.

The old crone pretends to think little of dress,
    But she practices just the reverse.
She encourageth pomp, she reproveth distress,
It is mostly the rich whom she deigns to caress,
And to keep in her favor requires nothing less
    Than a chronic discharge from the purse.

For virtue she gives a hysterical shriek,
    As if she alone could be good ;
But were the old walls of her wash-house to speak,
You would blush to be told human flesh is so weak.
And a few of her scrapes,—for frail vessels will leak—
    Are matters quite well understood.

And as for her boys, though they seem most devout,
    They're the slyest scape-graces in town ;
Fat living has rendered them greasy and stout,
They adore pretty women, they can't do without,
Every day some fresh scandal is going about
    Which their mother tries hard to keep down.

But she still goes on washing with might and with main,
    As if with some rival to cope.
In a liquid whose nature I cannot explain
She plungeth her duds, flecked with many a stain,
And she moaneth, and groaneth, and seemeth in pain,
    And is frequently yelling for ''soap !''

The old dame sets up a particular claim
   To what some denounce as a sham,—
For of quack advertising she knows the whole game,—
It's a " washing made easy," a fluid whose aim
Is to lessen the work, and, to give it a name,
   She has christened it " Bludovthalam."

In a very big Book she preserves the receipt,
   With advice and directions of worth ;
She claims the sole use, right and title complete.
Vows that all other compounds are only a cheat,
That hers, the original, cannot be beat—
   It's the greatest time-saviour on earth.

Testimonials many she shows which assert
   What wonders this fluid hath wrought ;
From a thief's filthy jacket it took all the dirt,
Removed the dark stains from a cyprian's skirt,
And made white as snow a foul murderer's shirt,
   All done with the quickness of thought.

If you ask my opinion of statements like these,
   I admit in plain terms that I doubt ;
I don't say they're lies, though they might be, with ease ;
They're illusions, vagaries, of divers degrees ;
Any sane court of common, or uncommon, pleas,
   Would rule all such evidence out.

But suppose they were true, to this point I will stick,
   'Tis a system unfair and unwise ;
Against honest toil 'tis a rascally kick,
It rots decent goods to go through them so quick ,
Some will hug their soiled duds 'till with dirt they are thick
To resort, when made sick, to this magical trick—
   These are facts which no art can disguise.

That this fluid saves labor I do not deny,
   But that is its limited scope ;
The things don't look clean when they're hung up to dry—
The dirt seems rubbed in, not rubbed out, to my eye,

It requires for the process whole oceans of LYE
   And immense contributions of " soap."

To have your things pure, sweet and fit to be seen,
   Don't go like a pilgrim—to roam ;
Don't send them away to be done by machine,
Or electrical fluid ; pray don't be so green ;
As long as you can, keep them spotlessly clean,
   Then carefully wash them at home.

Years ago I confess this old dame for a time
   I employed, by persuasion of friends ;
But I found that her fluid was not worth worth a d ime
To take out the rust and the grease and the grime,
So I left her, but still, as in youth's verdant prime,
   She her cards and her circulars sends.

Though against me her anger undoubtedly burns,
   She is hopeful of winning me back ;
When we meet she tries mildness and menace by turns,
She assures me her bosom unceasingly yearns,
But I know when her ultimate failure she learns,
   She will stamp me indelibly black.

If errors of life she is able to trace,
   On them she will grossly enlarge ;
She will sniff at my tracks like a hound in the chase,
Renew the sad blots I have tried to efface,
She will drag some poor skeleton out of its case,
And conclusively show that the vilest disgrace
   May correctly be laid to my charge.

Or, failing in that, with refreshing disdain
   She will promptly pronounce me a fool,
Or insist that I am and was always insane,
Or that habits of drink have disordered my brain;
That reason has wholly relinquished her reign,
   And tumbled flat off from her stool.

What she says, what she thinks, do not trouble me much,
    The time has gone by for alarm ;
I feel a bit safer when free from her clutch,
For her claws though cut short are still sharp to the touch,
But the legal restrictions at present are such,
    She can do me no bodily harm.

There are stories afloat, and no doubt they are true,
    Too awful almost to relate,
Of events which occurred when the laundry was new,
When to clear out her rivals this damnable shrew
Did not scruple her fingers with blood to imbrue,
    ·Inspired by demoniac hate.

She somehow got in with the powers of the day,
    And acquired the control of affairs ;
O'er the makers of laws she held absolute sway,
Even kings when she thumped on her board would obey;
Any soul who did washing, except in her way,
    Had short space for saying his prayers.

For those who had courage to stand in her path
    She made it excessively hot.
Their homes she surrendered to pillage and scath,
She branded their brows with the marks of her wrath,
Her furnaces ate them like kindlings of lath,
In her roaring big boilers she gave them a bath,
    And otherwise sent them to pot.

Come and see me some Sunday, of course after church,
    If a tithe of the facts you are told,
Which I have laid bare in my sorrowful search,
How, leaving truth, virtue and law in the lurch,
This vulture has climbed to her dignified perch,
    It will make your life-current run cold.

Go turn for yourself the grim volumes that stand
    On the dark, dusty bookshelves of time ;
If the walls of the wash-house, tall, solid and grand,

From roof to foundation were crumbled to sand,
Every grain might denote a foul page to be scanned
    For a separate story of crime.

These things are well known to her patrons and friends,
    Who partly acknowledge their truth ;
But declare that such acts as no person defends
Were mistakenly meant to secure some good ends,
And that years of repentance have furnished amends
    For the rash indiscretions of youth.

Though I fain would do justice, I cannot believe
    Her penitence aught than pretense;
Her crocodile tears are designed to deceive,
For while for her sins she professes to grieve,
She condemns some poor devil beyond all reprieve
    For a really more trifling offense.

Yet here at my low attic casement each day,
    In the brief blessed respites from toil,
I see fortune's children, the rich and the gay,
Togged out with bright jewels and costly array,
Drive up to the wash-house and then drive away,—
    What heaps of fine things they must soil.

And often at night in the glare of the gas
    The same rattling business goes on ;
Beyond the big windows, adorned with stained glass,
The regular customers pass and re-pass,
Their washing accumulates, mass upon mass,
And the merry old hopper keeps humming ; alas,
    How the dollars drop in and are gone !

Not only the plethoric pocket-books bleed,—
    She robs both the nabob and clown ;
The poor must pay tithes from the depths of their need,
Though their small jobs she mangles quite badly indeed,
They must pamper with pence her insatiate greed,
    Or incur the old termagant's frown.

If the money were spent at sweet charity's call,
    Which is sunk in this swindling machine,
No longer would poverty weigh like a pall,
Or ignorance fetter the land with its thrall ;
The sunlight of truth would give gladness to all,
    And the world be precisely as clean.

In the treadmills of toil, on the pitiless flags,
    Human misery grovels and grinds ;
In the trappings of shame, or the livery of rags,
With its babel of drunkards and harlots and hags,
Its tortuous slime o'er the nations it drags,
    Infecting whatever it finds.

There are schools to be founded, and homes to be built,
    There are babes to be sheltered and fed,
Young lives to be freed from contagion of guilt,
Holy war to be waged, ay, war to the hilt,
Where liquor, not blood, is the stream to be spilt,
    And mankind out of bondage be led.

There's a faith to be taught, a religion so pure,
    A seraph might own its control,—
Not a vulgar quack nostrum, sin-sickness to cure,
But a blessed soul-hygiene, unchanging and sure,
Whose principles grand cannot cease to endure
    While cycles uncounted shall roll.

Earth's children shall welcome the radiant gift,
    Which illumes the dark paths they have trod ;
A light pouring down through the Heavenly rift,
Not a glimpse to degrade to humanity's drift
The glory above, but to tenderly lift
    Men's thoughts like a vapor toward God.

Toward God,—but not him who, this creature pretends,
    As the first of her patrons is placed,
Who treats her as most confidential of friends,
Who whatever she asks for unthinkingly sends,
Who abhors what she merely dislikes, and commends
    Every notion that tickles her taste.

There is no such God ; to the reason of man
  He is only a bugbear, a myth.
To suppose that with him all creation began,
That his limited power can this universe span,
And control the vast scope of this infinite plan,—
  One might as well say it was SMITH.

The God I adore is a Being of awe,
  Whose person or sex none can trace ;
Not the bogy old Moses declared that he saw,
Not an ogre of wrath with omnivorous maw,
Not the chief of a sect, as blind egotists draw,
But the God of all beauty, of life, and of law
  Which no mortal can change or displace.

My God is to me more sublime than the sun
  To the dirt-digging ant of the plain,—
Paternal yet incomprehensible One,
Whose presence no atom of matter can shun,
From whom every stream of existence doth run,
And to whom it returns when its mission is done,
  As the rivulets flow to the main.

He shouts in the tempest, He lisps in the breeze,
  He chirps in the cricket's gay song ;
He paints on the leaves of the flowers and the trees,
He smiles in the sunshine, He laves in the seas,
In the dew-drop He weeps, and He sends his decrees
  As the planets go flashing along.

In the grand book of nature we read of God's power,
  But more of His wonderful love ;
It breathes in the fragrance of foliage and flower,
It warbles in songs from the tree-top and bower,
It sobs in the waves, and in moonlight's calm hour
  Its benison bends from above.

He abides everywhere, in the earth, in the air,
  And the limitless regions of space ;
If we follow and find the lost star, He is there,

Yet here at my window He ruffles my hair ;
Every night I resign my tired limbs to His care,
And my soul, too devout for articulate prayer,
   Is absorbed in His goodness and grace.

Oh, why should I pray to a Being so wise,
   As if with His wisdom to cope ?
Can I dream that my selfish petition would rise,
And bend to my fancy the King of the skies ?
Such an impudent thought, in no matter what guise,
I abandon to those who can gulp the fat lies
   Of the parson, the priest, and the pope.

Let me learn to be meek ; in the still summer night
   The glow-worm gropes round in the damp,
And out of his body emits a dim light,
Which brings a small circle of space to his sight,
But beyond, in the gloom, too remote for his flight,
   How futile the beams of his lamp.

Yet less than the insect that blinks in the grass
   Is man in creation's vast field.
He throws his dull rays on some things as they pass,
But beyond his low range is the principal mass,—
The gravest of sages is only an ass
   In describing what God has concealed.

Far away, where the sun of our system is seen
   As a spark in the ocean of blue,
If in worlds upon worlds floating calm and serene,
There are mountains and rivers and valleys of green,
And creatures like us to inhabit the scene,
They are surely my brothers and sisters, I ween,
   For the Parent I own is theirs too.

He is Father and Mother, Beginning and End,
   On His breast like a babe I recline ;
Though His purpose and plan I may not comprehend,
He has made me and cannot be aught but my friend ;
I will love Him and trust Him whate'er He may send;

In this life or another my path cannot wend
   From His presence and guidance divine.

I ponder these things as I sit here alone,
   When the lights in the laundry have fled ;
With the queen of the sky on her silvery throne,
And the stars that have watched as the ages have flown,
The great heart of nature comes close to my own,
And my spirit responds to the deep monotone
   Which resounds through the arches o'erhead.

And as on my brow fall the soft dews of night,
   Soft as memories of happier years,
So into my heart with a power to requite
The dry duties of life, fall the dews of delight,
And they swell to my eyes till they dim their glad sight
   With the blessed baptism of tears.

And over my soul creeps an infinite calm
   Which banishes hatred and doubt ;
At the specter of death I would feel no alarm,
God's messenger, bearing not wormwood but balm ;
The forces of nature can work me no harm
When embraced by their master's omnipotent arm,
   And supported within and without.

As I think of God's greatness and goodness, I feel
   What language can never convey;
I am lost in the love His creations reveal,
And I bow to His laws with devotion so leal,
And a heart so alive to humanity's weal,
That I almost forget or forgive the bad zeal
   Of the wash-woman over the way.

A LOCK OF HAIR.

Only a tress of dark brown hair,
A trifling gift from a lady fair,
Only a slender, circling strand,
Twined and tied by her own soft hand
'Tis pretty, yes, but we often fling
Thoughtlessly by, as pretty a thing,
Yet no mortal could rightly guess   .
The worth to me of this simple tress.

Far away, where the starlight sleeps
On verdant valleys and wooded steeps,
With night and silence to guard her rest,
Dwells the lady whom I love best.
She, in her cottage of quiet brown,
I, in the midst of the noisy town ;
Contrast sad and strange to see
Between the lady I love and me.

Over the pillow soft and white,
Glimmering faint in the dim starlight,
While she sleepeth, my lady fair,
Stray the locks of her dark brown hair.
Sleep, my darling, in peace sleep on,
Dream of the little tress that's gone ;
Dream of the lover whose fond lips press
The dear memento with mute caress.

Another form is reposing there,
Husband is he of my lady fair ;
To him the casket though I resign,
Her soul, the jewel of life, is mine.
God forgive us, he is my friend,
His trust, her honor, I must defend ;
Calm and constant his love has been,
My love is the feverish thirst of sin.

When through her window the morning breaks,
When with her household my love awakes,
Rose-lipped children will come to share
Kisses sweet from my lady fair.
Beautiful mother, her smiles are fond,
But, oh, their rapture were far beyond
If she, to the shame of the world unknown,
In those young features could see my own.

To gaze forever across the brink
Of pleasure's goblet, but not to drink,
To see the nectar I long to taste
Carelessly tippled or left to waste,
To know my love pines in her silken net,
This, this is torture, but keener yet
To think that my rival is sometimes pressed
With transient passion to her warm breast.

Was it for this, as the years have rolled,
I have turned toward woman an aspect cold?
For this have I struggled by day, by night,
In the world's hard battle to win the fight?
There are scars and furrows in heart and face,
And my life has shrunk to such narrow space,
Its proudest triumphs have grown so small
This dark brown circle enfolds them all.

Here, in the midnight hushed and deep,
Over my treasure strict watch I keep,
Clasp it close to my aching heart,
Never, till death, to be torn apart.
He alone who ruleth above
Can know the infinite pangs of love,
Of passionate yearning and dumb despair
That lurk, sometimes, in a lock of hair.

NEW TESTS FOR THE NEW TESTAMENT.

I love at times the good old Jesus story,
　　　　　—Jesus story,
Though perhaps it's getting now a trifle stale,
　　　　　—trifle stale,
But it seems to me the credit and the glory,
　　　　　—and the glory,
Should be placed upon a graduated scale,
　　　　　—on a scale.
The Pope is partly right, there's no denying,
　　　　　—no denying,
While the Protestants, poor beggars, are at sea,
　　　　　—are at sea.
All the bigots, big and little, have been lying,
　　　　　—have been lying,
But they can't inject their nonsense into me,
　　　　　—into me.

I've been reading up the business of the Passion,
　　　　　—of the Passion,
And I find with a disgust I can't disguise,
　　　　　—can't disguise,
For ages it has been the priestly fashion,
　　　　　—priestly fashion,
To scatter dust in simple people's eyes,
　　　　　—people's eyes.
Some very worthy persons have been slandered,
　　　　　—have been slandered,
While others have been treated with neglect,
　　　　　—with neglect,
If I raise them to their right and proper standard,
　　　　　—proper standard,
It is all my modest genius can expect,
　　　　　—can expect.

How much we owe the Blessed Virgin Mary,
                            —Virgin Mary,
Quite as much as Father, Son or Holy Ghost,
                            —Holy Ghost,
For had the dear old darling been contrary,
                            —been contrary,
In hell we all would surely have to roast,
                            —have to roast.
To her the papists bow in adoration,
                            —adoration,
And they know precisely what they are about,
                            —they're about ;
Without her the great scheme of man's salvation,
                            —man's salvation,
'Would undoubtedly have wholly fizzled out,
                            —fizzled out.

———

Of Joseph we have little information,
                            —information,
And to him full justice never has been done,
                            —has been done,
For he occupied a rather trusty station,
                            —trusty station,
As stepfather to Jehovah's only Son,
                            —only Son.
A smart rap from his maul of lignum vitæ,
                            —lignum vitæ,
Or a punch with his chisel's sharpened point,
                            —sharpened point,
And the wondrous plan devised by God Almighty,
                            —God Almighty,
Had at once been knocked completely out of joint,
                            —out of joint.

———

There is Judas, whom the parsons love to libel,
                            —love to libel,
Denouncing him as meaner than the rest,
                            —than the rest.

Of all the jolly blackguards in the Bible,
   —in the Bible,
I like cashier Iscariot much the best,
   —much the best.
Except for his most timely osculation,
   —osculation,
And his putting certain shekels in his fob,
   —in his fob,
The big contract of redemption and salvation,
   —and salvation,
Would have doubtless never been a finished job,
   —finished job.

———

P. Pilate, in his difficult position,
   —his position,
Displayed unusual forethought and good sense,
   —and good sense,
Though, being but a local politician,
   —politician,
He tried to keep on both sides of the fence
   —of the fence.
Had he listened to his weak wife's exhortation,
   —exhortation,
And tacked the thief Barabbas to the tree,
   —to the tree,
Every mother's son and daughter since Creation,
   —since Creation,
Would be damned, of course, including you and me,
   —you and me.

———

The Jews, who saved God's altars from pollution,
   —from pollution,
And to whom we owe His pure and Holy Word,
   —Holy Word,
Have been victims of religious persecution,
   —persecution,
For reasons and excuses most absurd,
   —most absurd.

I'm sick as rot of all this silly gabble,
    —silly gabble,
And the maudlin show of sentiment that's shammed,
    —that is shammed ;
Except for what they call the Jewish " rabble,"
    —Jewish " rabble,"
We good Christians would eternally be damned,
    —yes, be damned.

'Tis only through the life blood of the Saviour,
    —of the Saviour,
That our souls from sin are washed as white as wool,
    —white as wool ;
Then why accuse those chaps of misbehavior,
    —misbehavior,
Who secured the precious fluid free and full,
    —free and full.
Were it not for Christ's vicarious oblation,
    —His oblation,
Which supplied, as some would say, a long felt want,
    —long felt want,
There would be as slim a prospect of salvation,
    —of salvation,
As of Democratic triumph in Vermont,
    —in Vermont.

These verses may not equal some in beauty,
    —some in beauty,
But their meaning must be plainly understood,
    —understood ;
They are written from a pious sense of duty,
    —sense of duty,
And, egad, I hope they'll do a lot of good,
    —lot of good.
The world's great benefactors have been slandered,
    —have been slandered.
Or condemned to utter silence and neglect,
    —and neglect.
If I hoist them to their proper, normal standard,
    —normal standard,
'Tis as much as one poor devil can expect,
    —can expect.

29

THE SOLID HEADED PIN.

A MIXTURE OF RHYME AND REASON.

[NOTE.—It may interest some readers to be made acquainted
with the origin of these verses. A young lady of somewhat
liberal principles challenged the author to write a poem specially
for herself. The challenge being accepted, she was invited to
furnish a subject. She at once drew a pin from a cushion near
by and handed it to the author, remarking : "Here is a subject for you, which, though small, is quite pointed." The
author replied rather clumsily that he would proceed with his
appointed task, and hoped his fair friend would not be disap-
pointed with the result. The stanzas were soon after presented,
and the charming recipient testified her appreciation of them
by rewarding the author with a solid headed gold scarf pin.
Passing from hand to hand, a portion of this effusion eventually
found its way into the columns of an obscure country journal.
The editor, however, considered it his duty to make several
improvements, and by a process of literary emasculation rendered the verses as harmless and vapid as a hard shell Baptist
sermon without the usual modicum of sulphur. They are now
published for the first time in unmutilated form. The dedica-
tion which accompanied them in the original manuscript is
omitted for obvious reasons.]

Queer pins they had in days of yore,—
Such pins perchance your mother wore
When she was but a tiny elf ;
I've seen those little things myself.
The head and shaft were formed apart,
And joined with such imperfect art,
That, like a swain by Cupid led,
The pin would often lose its head.
Full forty years have passed away,
And if beneath your dress to-day
I search, those sacred folds within
I find the solid headed pin.

A quenchless thirst for rhyme you claim,—
I own a fondness for the same ;
I keep the poets on the shelf,
And write some little things myself.
To classic lore I don't pretend,—
The nineteenth century, my friend,
Can not its serious thoughts engage
With myths three thousand years of age.
No slobbery gush dilutes my song,
I like my verse and coffee strong ;
On common sense I stake and win—
I am a solid headed pin.

I want no dirty, slimy brutes
To daub their spittle o'er my boots,
I take the brushes from the shelf
And do those little things myself.
No corner artist's sable shine
Displays a finer gloss than mine,
And exercise like this, though brief,
Assists me to enjoy my beef.
Yet, being generously inclined,
To human curs I'm often kind,
And honest want attracts my tin —
I am a solid headed pin.

The barber's chair I don't frequent,
I reek not with his filthy scent ;
No cup of mine adorns his shelf—
I do those little things myself.
A strap makes boys and razors keen—
I keep my soap and brushes clean ;
No itch my smiling chaps betray,
O'er my smooth skin no vermin play.
I shun the greasy, chattering clan,
And place their nostrums under ban ;
We do without each other's " chin,"—
I am a solid headed pin.

I have a wife and children three,
The youngsters all resemble me ;
No rival claims on one sweet elf—
I do those little things myself.
I go not to the club or play
And leave my wife at home to stay ;
The opera she does not attend
Escorted by my trusted friend.
When marriage vows are brought to shame
There's often more than one to blame,—
The best way out is, don't get in ;
I am a solid headed pin.

I train not with the temperance bands,
I wear no shackles on my hands.
I keep good liquors on the shelf,
And mix some little things myself.
Yet, when I drink I sing no hymn
Nor cite old Paul's remarks to Tim ;
I see no harm in beer or punch,
Regarded as a fluid lunch.
At home I sip whene'er I choose,
But not where sots and bummers booze ,
With me no blackguard swills his gin—
I am a solid headed pin.

We're sometimes sick, but then you see
A panic never seizes me ;
With jars and bottles on the shelf
I fix some little things myself.
A sweat full oft subdues a chill,
I'm competent to give a pill,
It needs no surgeon's dextrous knack
To slap a plaster on one's back.
My wife has sense ; she don't propose
For tickling in the baby's nose,
With drugs to fill his precious skin,—
She is a solid headed pin.

The bulldog's bloody teeth may slip—
Not so the law's tenacious grip ;
With blanks and form-books on the shelf,
I do a bit of law myself.
At school I learned to read and write,
I put all things in black and white ;
From brawls and debts I hold aloof,
And quote no tale that lacks the proof.
I may admire a handsome trap,
And not object to hear it snap,
But pray excuse my tender shin,
I am a solid headed pin.

I know a pack of cards can be
Productive of much harmless glee ;
You'll always find them on my shelf—
I like a little game myself.
But if I play for stakes at all,
The sums must be extremely small;
No healthy appetite requires
Excitement to sustain its fires.
In gambling dens I do not range,
Not even in the Stock Exchange ;
I see the shark's protruding fin,—
I am a solid headed pin.

On Sunday no abode of grace
Is shocked to see my jovial face ;
For guesses wild I pay no pelf,—
I do those little things myself.
No gospel sharp can gain control,
And place a mortgage on my soul,—
Of goblin worlds he need not try
To tell, he knows no more than I.
Unless the day is cold or dark,
I take my darlings to the park,
And talk of nature, not of sin,—
I am a solid headed pin.

Thus I, with my beloved wife,
Pursue a philosophic life ;
Ambitious not for power or pelf,
I speak, and act, and am, myself.
I bend no knee at fashion's throne,
No collar wear, except my own ;
A czar will rule this country when
A muzzle curbs my tongue or pen.
As I have lived so I shall die,
And o'er my bones a slab you'll spy,
With this inscription scratched therein :
HERE STICKS A SOLID HEADED PIN.

WATER LILIES.

Out of the darkness into the light,
Up from the dreary realm of night,
Through thick curtains of ooze and slime,
Up, still upward, the lilies climb.
Closing their lips and holding their breath,
Higher and higher at each day's death,
Yearning to bask in the light sublime,
Up, still upward, the lilies climb.

All the heavens are blue and bright,
Down in the depths of my soul is night ;
Lilies of hope are trying to rise
To be kissed by the winds and cloudless skies.
Secretly hiding their fragrance and bloom,
Oh, shall they ever, through grief and gloom,
Open their petals, so pure and white,
Out of the darkness, in love's glad light ?

Lady fair, with your blue, blue eyes,
In your smiles there are cloudless skies,
In sweet words from your lips that flow
Winds of Eden breathe soft and low.
Be it folly or fate or crime,
Upward to you my hopes will climb,
And you alone can those hopes invite
Out of the darkness and into the light.

OLD JOKES MADE VERSE.

I.

A famed physician
   Who flourished years and years ago—
Perhaps you need not know
   His name or age or previous condition—
Lived in a thriving town out West
   In a respectable, substantial manner ;
Exactly where might possibly be guessed,
   But is not an important quest ;
To make the rhyme
   Without unnecessary waste of time,
Let's call it Indiana.

His was acknowledged skill ;
   Of potion, powder, plaster, poultice, pill,
And remedies for every ill,
   This learned doctor
Was an experienced concocter.
   But, equal to his medical renown,
His gruff deportment and profanity—
   Sometimes approaching inhumanity,
Were known to all the town.

One freezing winter night
   A luckless, dissipated wight,
Of home and friends bereft,
   And not a single shilling left
With which to rent a bed,
   No place to lay his head,—
In wandering about,
   Half drunk, no doubt,
Perceived all lights were out,
   Excepting one ; a luminous expansion
From one high window shone,
   With lustre all its own,
And that was in the doctor's mansion.

'Twas midnight's holy hour,
   The stars were coldly shining,
He felt their solemn power
   Impress his soul with sad repining.
But as his coat was innocent of lining,
   He felt still more the eager wind
Which through his threadbare garments stole
   By many a hole;
And leaving formal etiquette behind,
   Attracted by the hospitable candle,
He quit the cheerless street,
   Approached the door-step with unsteady feet,
Crept up and pulled the handle.

Clang ! went the bell within,
   Awakening a horrid din.
The doctor started from his deep,
   Sonorous sleep,
And to the partner of his bosom said :
   " Good God ! another call,—I swear
This devilish night work's more than I can bear."
   Then getting out of bed,
Straight to the window he advanced,
   Threw up the sash and downward glanced.

Seeing upon the icy stone
   A figure grim and gaunt,
He cried in surly tone :
   " Hello, there, what in hell d'ye want ?"
The tramp his irate questioner then eyed,
   And in a voice made thick with drink replied,
" I want to stay here—hic !—all night."
   The doctor yelled, " All right,—
You're welcome quite,
   Just stay there and be damned ! "
And down the window slammed.

II.

A banker of very great wealth, it is told,
   But of quite economical views,
As he sat in his counting-house, fondling his gold,
   Was appealed to one day, by a mendicant bold,
For an old pair of trousers or shoes.

"Go away, stupid fellow," the banker replied,
   As he turned on the man with a sneer,
" In this narrow place do you think I abide .
   Go away," he repeated with arrogant pride,
" I don't keep my wardrobe in here ! "

The beggar rejoined with a broad Irish grin,
   "Wan favor an thin I'll be gone ;
Jist say where yez live an as sartin as sin
   I'll call there to-morrer to see if yer in,
An git thim owld duds ye have on ! "

III.

"I'm fond of fresh hair," the Englishman said,
   Then to make his remark more clear,
He added, " I mean, not the 'air of the 'ead,
   But the hair of the hatmosphere."

IV.

" I hate tobacco," said Tom's sire,—
   His brow grew dark with grief and ire ;
"What can be your excuse
   When thus to me you give no heed,—
What makes you chew the filthy weed ?"
   Quoth Tom, " To get the juice ! "

V.

" Why Bridget," said she, " this is really shocking,
   Can it be that the coffee you strain through a stocking ?
Such an act on your part seems to me an insane one ! "
   " Shure, mum," replied Bridget, " It isn't a clane one ! "

VI.

'Tis said that figures cannot lie,—
The ancient statement I deny,
And place my proof in sight.
On this arrangement cast your eye:
1 2 3 4 5 6 7 8 9
See how these figures flatly lie,—
Not one remains upright.

VII.

"Parents," the solemn man spoke out,
"Children you have beyond a doubt,
Or will have at some future day,—
If not, perhaps your daughters may."

VIII.

The man who in business would thievishly think,
To thrive with the public without printer's ink,
Resembleth the ardent but diffident spark
Who winketh sly winks at a girl in the dark.
He knoweth, no doubt, what he is about,
But nobody else ever findeth it out.

IX.

Says Dr. Bones to Parson Jones,
"To cure you of that dumb ache
Let me advise, take exercise
Upon an empty stomach."
Then moans poor Jones, in plaintive tones,
"On whose, pray tell me, Dr. Bones?"

X.

Said fair Miss Hyde to Mr. Finn,
"Sir, can you play the violin?"
Said Mr. Finn to fair Miss Hyde,
"I do not know, I never tried."

TWO BIRTHDAYS.

Nineteen to-night,—in the changeful flight
   Of seasons coursing on tireless wings,
The waning ray of a dull March day
   To Flora another birthnight brings.
She sits in the gloom of the unlit room,
   And her voice floats out in a plaintive lay,
But her pure young heart, from the song apart,
   Is with its master and far away.

One year to-night there was mirth and light,
   And wit and beauty made glad the scene ;
A maiden fair with dark brown hair
   Was tasting the freedom of sweet eighteen.
Twelve months have flown, and to-night, alone,
   A matron sits in the twilight gray,
Ano she sings a strain with a sad refrain,
   Which tells of a dear one far away.

Not only of him are the thoughts that swim
   In the musical dream of the matron fair,—
In the shadowy morn of a joy new born
   Her heart trills a softer, diviner air.
There's a hope that swells, and a love that wells
   From depths too sacred for passion's sway,—
She may sing ere long a lullaby song
   To a dear little stranger not far away.

Sing on, true heart ; wherever thou art,
   Thy song shall breathe of a purer life,
Of a love that clings to the simple things
   Which crown with honor the name of wife.
Sing on, love on,—and when Heaven shall dawn,
   And your voice be tuned to an angel lay,
I pray you may meet your loved ones sweet,
   And sigh for none who are far away.

DEARER BY GOD, TO THEE.
(*Dedicated to Bister Boody.*)
BY A GOOD BAD.

[NOTES.—The reader may observe that in some of the later
stanzas of this hymn, certain words have been omitted to facili-
tate the adaptation to music ; but care has been exercised that
the sense of the lines shall not be materially changed. With
many of the standard hymns of the Church greater liberties
have been taken, and the original meaning sacrificed to the
supposed necessities of the meter. This is not a fair shake,
and in the author's forthcoming collection of religious songs,
the Holy Roly Poly and Gospel Hurdy Gurdy, no such viola-
tions of good taste will be permitted.

As the present hymn is too long for general occasions, it
may be suggested that for most purposes it would be advisable
to select the first, fourth and last stanzas, and omit the others.
The author, however, trusts he may be allowed to say that a
perusal of the whole of the poem is necessary for a complete
understanding of its motive. It is designed to portray the
pious hopes and devout aspirations of the average Christian of
the period, disgusted with feeding on the dry husks of unprofit-
able sin, and though not unmindful of the good things of this
world, looking confidently forward to the honor of being
among the select few at his Father's table, where, to carry out
the familiar and favorite metaphor, he can have everything of
first-class quality, cooked to order, and served in Delmonico
style.

This beautiful hymn is evidently intended to be sung with
catarrh accompaniment.]

Dearer, by God, to thee,
Dearer to thee ;
If sidders will be dabbed
What's that to be ?
If they like sulphur sbell
Let theb all go to hell ;
Where saidts ad adgels dwell
Bore roob for Be !

I was a sidder wudce,
  Berry ad gay,—
Very fast, bad youg bad,
  So people say.
But as the years wedt od,
With health ad buddy god,
This truth begad to dawd,
  Sid did dot pay.

Dow I'b a pious bad,
  Say dothig wrog ;
Od Sudday go to church,—
  Face a yard log.
Give to hobe bissiods free—
Let all the people see !
"Dearer, by God, to thee,"
  By codstadt sog.

Dearer, by God, to thee,
  Dearer to thee ;
Let be, Lord, tickle you,
  You tickle be.
By dabors hear be pray
Every dight ad every day,—
They see it's all O. K.
  'Twixt you ad be.

Whed I ab here do bore,
  Whed life is dud,
Please let Be be a God—
  Just a sball wud.
Give be a little throde,
Bade for by use alode,
With adgels of by owd,—
  That would be fud !

Thed id by Heavedly hobe
  Happy I'll be ;
It will be just like wud
  Eterdal spree.

I will bake old harp rig,
I will dadce, yell ad sig,
Dearer, Albighty Kig,
   Dearer to thee.

If what the parsods say
   All turds out true,
Heav'd bust be gay old place,
   For Be—ad you.
But perhaps I should sbile—
It bust be out of style ;—
Give be the order, I'll
   Fit it up dew.

Dearer, by God, to thee,
   Dearer to thee ;
I've stuck to you, by God,
   You bust to be.
After all lies I've crabbed,
All gooddess I have shabbed,
If you let Be be dabbed,
   You are " Ed G ! "

JEST-NUTS.

A DELICATE COURTESY.

Your writing is bad, but it makes me feel glad,
  Its tremor I quite understand ;
You merely intend, as a long absent friend,
  To give me the shake of your hand.

Opposites Attract. Among the vane things of this world, the weather-cock is perhaps the most vacillating of birds ; and yet the object to which it is strongly attached is almost always stable.

A clerk in a store where kerosene is sold at retail, may properly be said to occupy a serve-ile position.

Similia similibus curantur. The Pilgrim's Progress was produced by a Bunyan ; and every pedestrian tourist will assure you that a bunion is often produced by the pilgrim's progress.

The acrobat, like death, has all seasons for his own. Even in winter he may indulge in a gentle spring, take a little summer-sault, and if not careful, get an early fall.

It is a singular but undeniable fact that umbrellas are of most service when they are used up, and overshoes when they are worn out.

You've seen that pretty opera,
  The " Pirates of Penzance ; "
No language could be properer
  For metrical romance.
To say the piece has vulgar strains
  No surly critic dares,
And yet it certainly contains
  A number of cors-airs.

CUPID'S VAGARIES.

Some lovers lean to beauties slim,
    With bony-fide adoration ;
Some suetors show a diffcrent whim,
    And find in fat infatuation.
This serves to prove that love, like sin,
Can live and thrive through thick and thin.

——— —

There are many arduous labors connected with the life of a clergyman, and yet it may be said that he has charge of a sinner-cure.

——— —

"Autumn leaves"—November 30th.

——— —

This beats all. What is the difference between a dead dead beat and a live dead beat? One lies still and the other still lies.

——— —

Should peerless beauties peer less in pier-glasses,
    They would appear less vain of charms they view ;
Should peers and plebeians peer less in beer-glasses,
    There'd be less beer, and many a bier less, too.

——— —

Why are two hundred and eighty-eight copies of the Old Testament unfit for publication? Because they arc two gross.

——— —

As pork is not a Jew dish, can its use be considered judicious?

——— —

Can a scholar reasonably expect to rise by getting lore?

——— —

FAVORITE SONGS.

The milkmaid's song : " I have learned to love an udder."
The whaler's song : " Beautiful ile of the sea."
The baker's song : " I knead thee every hour."
Song of the lisping young lády to her lover : " Oh, how happy could I be with thee, thir."
Song of the shepherd—" The ewe'll remember me."

DEFINITIONS.

Party measures—the music at a reception.
Unexpected recovery—a returned umbrella.
The town crier—an almshouse baby.
A strong limb—Limberger.
A light mist—a blown-out candle.
Cold steal—robbing an ice-cart.
Chest protectors—safe deposit companies.
Lay figures—statistics of the egg crop.
A healthy beverage—well water.
A tight fit—an attack of delirium tremens.
Death caused by imperfect drainage—sewerside.
A noose-paper—a marriage certificate.

When is water like a good picture ?   When it is well-drawn.

A book-keeper in church is the write man in the rite place.

To what government do the Turks owe allegiance?   Why, to the Porte, you geese.

What is the difference between an apothecary and a plantation hand ?   One is a pharmacist, the other a farm assistant.

MIRACLES MADE EASY.

To turn water into wine,—dilute your claret.

To raise the dead,—join a resurrectionist party of medical students.

To make the deaf hear,—make a disparaging remark about him in his presence.

To make the lame walk,—take him to the theatre and get some fool in the gallery to yell "fire !"

To make the blind see,—let him fall on the ice with full force on the back of his head.   He will immediately see stars.

To feed the multitude with five loaves and two stale fishes,—announce a first-class free lunch of oysters, boned turkey, chicken salad, ice cream, &c., to occur later.

LINES—BY OLD SMITH.

When, lured by agent's oily fallacy,
    A good, well-meaning man some day
Takes a big life-insurance policy,
    And finds the premiums hard to pay,—
 . The only plan which seems judiciary,
    For such sad wight to profit by,
Quite sure to please his beneficiary,
    And stop the payments is—to die.

" Heaven lies about us in our infancy," says Wordsworth ;
and he might have added, that the world usually lies about us
when we are grown up.

A door is said to be fast—when it is bolted ; a dinner is
eaten too fast—when it is bolted ; an eloping wife is supposed
to be fast—when she has bolted.

RELIGIOUS EVOLUTION.

The Church, in this progressive age,
    Is changed in names, if not in nature ;
Its shrewd, time-serving managers
    Have softened down its nomenclature.

No more they preach eternal HELL,
    To shock the ears of youths and ladies ;
But sometimes, in an undertone,
    Politely speak of Hades.

Sinners of old were DAMNED, by God,
    Who poured His wrath in stintless measure ;
But now the worst that can befall
    Is to incur " Divine displeasure."

If this goes on, in course of time,
    When things shall reach their final level,
They'll make the " pit " a pious place,
    And canonize the Devil.

THE LESSON OF LIFE.

Adown the ceaseless stream of years
　Our fragile barks are swiftly flying ;
Childhood like some vague dream appears,
　Its voices in the distance dying ;
Spring's hope and Summer's promise fade,
　Awhile the wealth of Autumn lingers,
Then Winter, solemnly arrayed,
　Folds down the shroud with icy fingers.

'Tis well unwelcome changes creep
　In imperceptible succession,
The spoiler's blows may wound us deep,
　And yet we know no rude impression ;
We cannot feel our heart-throbs flag,
　We cannot trace the wrinkles coming,
In measured march our steps we drag,
　Nor catch the players' muffled drumming.

We shall not all survive our youth,
　For some grim Death his scythe is whetting ;
Though angels hide the awful truth,
　For some the sun is almost setting.
But since the end we cannot see,
　At duty's call we each should rally,
Unheedful of how short shall be
　Our journey toward the quiet valley.

Time past is useless save to teach
　The lessons needed in the present;
'Tis vain to weave the song or speech
　From vanished moments, sad or pleasant;
There's work and wages for us all,
　Earth's harvest fields await our reaping;
The past is lost beyond recall,—
　We hold the future in our keeping.

In every life some crises rise,
  Some moments grasping years within them ;
Fierce conflicts come, and he is wise
  Who wears a warrior garb to win them.
One breath along the serried line
  Scarce may be heard a saber's rattle,
The next all heaven and earth combine
  To swell the crash, the roar of battle.

We live in thought and word and deed,
  Not in the changes of the dial ;
That life is brief, though gray with greed,
  Which bears no fruit of toil and trial.
Long prayers are vain if lacking still
  The works that to fulfilment bring them,
Loud hymns of labor serve but ill
  To sit with folded hands and sing them.

The sermon in this simple lay
  Full oft the voice of nature broaches ;
In the world's vineyard work to-day,
  Work, for the night of death approaches.
Work with your hands, your tongue, your pen,
  No soul is sunk below your reaching ;
Teach purer, nobler lives to men,
  And act the spirit of your teaching.

Waste not your breath in war of creeds,
  'Tis but a choice of superstitions;
Truth is the bread for human needs,
  Not the stale drugs of priest-physicians.
Gods change,—the fetich of to-day
  Shall yield his scepter to another,
But man remains the same for aye,
  While ages roll he is your brother.

At death's dark door a veil is drawn,—
  We may not lift its somber trailing;
Why stand with backs against the dawn

And strive with guesses unavailing?
Hark! down the vista of the years
  Faint music thrills with deep vibrations,
And blended with its notes one hears
  The tramp of future generations.

Their pickets, swarming in our track,
  Familiar seem, with kindred mission,
But, following closely at their back,
  Strange faces mock our recognition.
Strange armor glistens in the sun,
  Strange songs arise in concert solemn,
And farther than our thoughts can run
  Sweeps on the broadening, endless column.

Brave prophets of the coming time,
  Above the strife of fraud and faction
Ring out the words whose power sublime
  Shall rouse earth's sons to grander action.
Hasten the dawn of that bright day
  Whose beams shall drive the mists of error,
And man, beneath mild reason's sway,
  Be ruled by love, and not by terror.

Brother, endowed with heart and brain,
  Of selfish aims throw off the fetter;
Within some certain realm you reign,
  And you can make things vastly better.
In purpose, love and faith be strong,
  And though fame's wreath may crown you never,
Yet in truth's final triumph song
  Shall swell the notes of your endeavor.

www.ingramcontent.com/pod-product-compliance
Lightning Source LLC
Chambersburg PA
CBHW021235260626
47172CB00002B/770